Jonas Sickler

W9-BCI-205

FRÈRE JACQUES

WORKMAN PUBLISHING · NEW YORK

FRÈRE JACQUES

Hey, baby! Look where Jacques is sleeping—and dreaming—in Paris!

JONAS SICKLER

THE MILLION-COPY SERIES

INDESTRUCTIBLES®

BOOKS BABIES CAN REALLY SINK THEIR GUMS INTO!

Frère Jacques, Frère Jacques,
Dormez-vous? Dormez-vous?
Sonnez les matines! Sonnez les matines!
Din, dan, don. Din, dan, don.

Are you sleeping? Are you sleeping?
Brother John, Brother John,
Morning bells are ringing! Morning bells are ringing!
Ding, dang, dong. Ding, dang, dong.

Dear Parents: INDESTRUCTIBLES are built for the way babies "read": with their hands and mouths. INDESTRUCTIBLES won't rip or tear and are 100% washable. They're made for baby to hold, grab, chew, pull, and bend.

Chew them all!

WORKMAN PUBLISH
225 Varick St
New York, NY 10
workman.com/indestructi

$5.95 U.S. ISBN 978-0-7611-59

Copyright © 2011 by Indestructibles, Inc. Used under license.
Illustrations copyright © 2011 by Jonas Sickler
Library of Congress Cataloging-in-Publication Data is available.
WORKMAN is a registered trademark of Workman Publishing Co., Inc.
First printing January 2011
10 9 8 7 6 5

All INDESTRUCTIBLES books have been safety-te
and meet or exceed ASTM-F963 and CPSIA guide
INDESTRUCTIBLES is a registered trademark of TyBoo
Contact specialmarkets@workman.com rega
special discounts for bulk purch
Printed in